# Forward, Shakespeare!

## Jean Little

ORCA BOOK PUBLISHERS

**National Library of Canada Cataloguing in Publication Data**

Little, Jean, 1932-
Forward, Shakespeare! / Jean Little.

(Orca young readers)
Sequel to: Rescue pup.
ISBN 1-55143-339-7

I. Title.  II. Series.

PS8523.I77F67 2005          jC813'.54          C2005-904615-5

First published in the United States, 2005
**Library of Congress Control Number:** 2005930966

**Summary:** In this sequel to *Rescue Pup*, Shakespeare, the unusual Seeing Eye dog who understands Human, must win over his new master, a desperately unhappy young man who was recently blinded in an accident.

Free teachers' guide available at www.orcabook.com

Orca Book Publishers gratefully acknowledges the support for its publishing programs provided by the following agencies: the Government of Canada through the Department of Canadian Heritage's Book Publishing Industry Development Program (BPIDP), the Canada Council for the Arts, and the British Columbia Arts Council.

Typesetting and cover design by Lynn O'Rourke
Cover & interior illustrations by Hanne Lore Koehler

**In Canada:**
Orca Book Publishers
Box 5626 Stn. B
Victoria, BC  Canada
V8R 6S4

**In the United States:**
Orca Book Publishers
PO Box 468
Custer, WA  USA
98240-0468

www.orcabook.com
Printed and bound in Canada.
08 07 06 • 6 5 4 3 2

*This story is dedicated to my Seeing Eye friend*
*Valerie Browne, and to Doug Roberts*
*and Pete Jackson, who taught me*
*how to work with my dog guides.*
*Thank you all from the bottom of my heart.*

# Chapter 1

As Shakespeare and his friend Larkin were driven away from the Benson farm, they had no notion what lay ahead.

*Why were Kevin and Tessa crying?* Larkin asked in Dog. Larkin was a black Labrador retriever.

*They're going to miss us,* Shakespeare told him. Shakespeare was the yellow Lab also known as Rescue Pup.

*But we'll be going home again, won't we?* Larkin demanded.

Shakespeare did not answer. They had lived with the Bensons and their foster children since they were mere puppies. Their memories of their babyhood at the Seeing

Eye were fuzzy and faint. Now they had been told they were going to become dog guides, but they did not really know what that meant.

Shakespeare could understand Human, the language used by people, as well as Dog, the telepathic speech with which canines communicated with each other. When he had been a small puppy, he had imagined that all dogs understood human speech, but he had soon learned that he was gifted with special powers. His extra ability had made him feel lonely at first, but by this time he was not only used to it but thankful for it. After all, it let him tell Larkin that they were going to school to learn to guide the blind. Even so, he was not sure what "blind" meant.

*What are "the blind"?* Larkin asked humbly, certain that his clever friend would have the answer ready.

Shakespeare gave him a baffled look.

*They talk about "the blind" a lot,* he said. *But nobody ever stops to explain what the words mean. We'll find out soon enough, I guess.*

Larkin stared at him.

*I thought you understood all their words,* he said.

*Not quite. But whatever "blind" means, it's not something bad; it's something important,* Shakespeare told him. *Tessa promised it would be an adventure.*

Larkin was not comforted. Tessa and Kevin, the Bensons' foster children, watched adventures on TV. Superheroes got into all sorts of danger on their adventures. Shakespeare might feel like Superdog, but Larkin did not. Remembering all the loud explosions and screams, he shivered.

Shakespeare saw him tremble and wanted to give his soft ear a sharp nip. Why was Larkin such a baby?

*It'll be fine,* Shakespeare said. *Don't quake. We can handle anything.*

Then they arrived at the Seeing Eye and the world grew suddenly familiar. Larkin gave a vast sigh of relief as Jonah took them back into the kennels that had once been their home. Shakespeare also relaxed. Home was now with Tessa, but the Seeing Eye still had the right smells and noises.

My first home, he thought. That's what this is.

He looked around for his mother, but she was nowhere to be seen. He was not too surprised. She was probably busy looking after a new litter of pups. Babies were not housed in this part of the kennel.

Then he heard his brother Skip barking a welcome, and his joyous tail whipped from side to side in response.

"Settle down, you guys," Jonah's voice commanded.

Skip hushed, and Shakespeare's tail waved even harder. Once when Shakespeare was small, Jonah had picked him up by the scruff of his neck and dangled him in space. But Jonah was part of his babyhood, and Shakespeare was pleased to hear his voice again.

"Hi, Shakespeare," Jonah said, grinning down at him. "I've been hearing great stories about you."

Shakespeare knew what he meant. After all, the Bensons had told everyone how special he was. "Rescue Pup," Peg Benson called him. He had only run for help when a falling tree limb had knocked Dan Benson out. But it had been harder than Mrs. Benson guessed because he had had to cross the creek that had almost drowned him when he was tiny. Still, he had done it, and Mr. Benson was fine now.

"I was proud," Jonah said, reaching to scratch behind a floppy blond ear.

Shakespeare leaned into the comfortable scratch. "Aw, shucks, it was nothing," he longed to say. But although he could understand Human, he couldn't speak a word of it. He looked down at his forepaws instead, as though he was embarrassed by the praise.

Jonah laughed aloud. "You're the same old Shakespeare, I see," he said. "Hi, Skip. Hello, Stormy. Good boy, Larkin."

He gave pats all around and turned to leave. Then he glanced back.

"It's hard to believe you're all so grown up," he said softly. "And soon you'll be put to the test. You'd think I would be used to it by now, but I am always amazed. Good luck. Be seeing you."

Even though Shakespeare missed Tessa sorely, that night back at the Seeing Eye was like a family reunion.

The next morning, the tests began. The dogs were examined from nose to tail by veterinarians. Their vision and their hearing were checked. Were the pads on their paws too sensitive? Did they get motion sick? Were they apt to start a fight? Were they ready to mix into one started by another dog? Were they timid or mean? Shakespeare, puzzled but willing, sailed through with flying colors.

"Your real training begins today," Jonah told him one morning. "Your teacher is the best. He'll turn you into a spectacular Seeing Eye dog."

What was a Seeing Eye dog? And what was a teacher?

Teach arrived then. He squatted and held out his hand for the dog to sniff. Shakespeare liked him at once. His voice was friendly and so was his smell.

"We have work to do, boy," the man said. "Important work. I know you can handle it."

Shakespeare listened hard for a moment. Then he wagged his tail furiously. Whatever came next, he was ready. He missed Tessa, but he knew something exciting was just ahead. He had no notion it was going to be a matter of life and death.

# Chapter 2

Jonah came by at that moment and stopped to chat.

"He's one smart dog," he told Teach. "Mrs. Benson told my mom that he changed a tough kid into a girl with a heart. He also ran for help when Mrs. Benson's husband was in some accident. She calls him Rescue Dog."

"Fine," Teach said, grinning at the excited pup with the impressive name. "Let's go, Rescue Dog."

At first Teach petted Shakespeare and talked to him. He had other dogs to train too. Shakespeare was overjoyed to find Larkin and Skip also in Teach's string.

"You boys look like twins," their teacher said, glancing at the two brothers.

Then Teach put a leather harness on Shakespeare and taught him to walk forward steadily in the harness. After that they walked through Morristown, getting familiar with parking meters, stores, traffic islands, coffee shops, parks, cats and squirrels.

"Leave it," Teach would say when Shakespeare sniffed a hedge or paused by a fire hydrant.

Then Shakespeare met his first pigeon. For one second, he froze. Then he realized that these birds were far smaller than Zorro, the attack rooster who had done his best to murder the pup. And Shakespeare was lots bigger than his puppy self. He looked down his nose at the poor feathered creatures and marched past without turning one golden hair.

Cars were another matter. The first time one seemed headed right for him, he jumped back, nearly knocking Teach over. He had seen Larkin struck by a car and was stiff with terror. He could not help it.

"Steady. Easy does it, Shakespeare. Let's try again," the man said, his voice calm.

And he walked the bewildered dog straight toward a busy street. He stopped at the curb. Cars passed, but none was intent on killing Shakespeare. The dog stood his ground. After all, he had ridden in cars. They were not the enemy. He grew calm again and walked willingly at his teacher's side.

Then Teach stumbled over a curb. Shakespeare pulled ahead, doing his best to encourage his new friend. Teach gave the leash a sharp yank.

"Phooey!" he snapped.

Shakespeare was puzzled. But he remembered Larkin's body flying through the air. He knew full well that traffic was dangerous. He began to stop when he saw a car coming. The next day, at the first corner, he saw no car but stopped anyway to be on the safe side.

"Phooey!" Teach began to say—and caught himself. He stared at the dog.

"Jonah was right," he muttered. "You are one smart pup."

Shakespeare learned to watch out for any peril, however minor, that bothered Teach. He learned not to let his mind wander. Whenever he did well, Teach behaved as though the dog had given him a juicy marrowbone.

"Good boy," he would croon. "Atta boy, Shakespeare."

Shakespeare was pleased with himself, but he tried not to let it go to his head. He had to concentrate. His teacher had told him so more than once.

Next Teach objected to leaves brushing his head. Shakespeare could not believe how fussy he was. Let a twig touch his hair and… "Phooey!" Jerk! Yank!

Then, just as they approached a thick branch, broken but dangling at head level, Shakespeare was distracted for a moment by a flurry of pigeons taking off after a lady with sandwich crusts in her hand.

*Whack!*

Teach clutched his head. A lump as big as a dog biscuit was coming up. His moan was worse than any "Phooey!" Poor guy.

Shakespeare finally understood what the fuss had been about. He started looking up and guiding Teach around overhead branches or signs. He never missed one again.

"He's incredible," Teach told the others.

When Shakespeare had learned to stop for all curbs, evade all obstacles, and when he could ignore rude dogs, friendly dogs, dogs he was in school with, fierce cats and passing pigeons, Teach began the hardest lesson of all.

"This next thing is tricky, boy. It's called 'intelligent disobedience.' Let's give it a try and see how you like it. Forward, Shakespeare," he ordered.

Sure he knew exactly what his teacher wanted, Shakespeare obeyed instantly even though a car was coming. Teach whacked the side of the car, yelled, "Phooey!" and gave the bewildered Lab a sharp leash correction.

Shakespeare had trouble with this. Obey, he reminded himself and kept going. Another leash correction! He looked up at his instructor and tried to puzzle out what he was after. Then Teach made it clear.

"You have to think," he said. "You have to obey unless your intelligence tells you only a fool would obey this time. Then you must refuse to move, dig in your claws and freeze until the person holding the harness handle smartens up. Intelligent disobedience it's called, remember. Forward."

Teach wanted him to disobey when the command would take them into big trouble! It made much more sense than obeying even when it would risk both their lives. Shakespeare gave his mind to it. Again, Teach was astonished when this dog understood what was meant so swiftly.

The other dogs got it fast as well, that is once they had spent the evening having it explained to them by Shakespeare.

*Why are we having to do all this training at all?* Skip wondered, shaking his head at the foolishness of humans. *These humans don't need us to keep them safe.*

*You wait. Teach will have a good reason. He's no dummy,* Shakespeare insisted.

A few days later, when they all seemed ready, Teach told them that the next day they would try something called "the blind-fold test."

Shakespeare did not know the word "blind-fold." He thought he had Human down pat, but he had missed that one. He watched Teach hide his eyes behind a sort of mask. He, Shakespeare, was going to have to guide a man who couldn't see. It did not make sense, but Shakespeare had faith in himself and his training. He knew, deep in his heart, that he and Teach could handle anything Morristown had to offer. He was excited. And he was right. They were a flaw-less team.

"You're ready, boy," Teach told him, "to meet your blind person. Now you will find out what all this training is in aid of. And we're giving you a kid who will test your mettle. His name is Tim. He's young to be getting a dog guide, and it wasn't his idea. He's con-vinced no canine, however well trained, can help him. I think he plans to fail here and go home without a dog. But I believe you will win him around. If you live up to your repu-tation, you should be perfect for him. Just bear in mind that you are the leader, and his job is to follow. You'll be fine."

Shakespeare had heard the word "blind" many times since coming to the Seeing Eye, but he had never grasped its meaning. He had known that he would be moving on, but he had no idea what was coming next. He did not want to be parted from Teach.

He was certainly not ready for the bitterly angry blind kid he was about to meet.

# Chapter 3

That Monday Jonah gave Shakespeare a needless bath before Teach took him down the hall to meet Tim. The Lab was curious. What exactly was a blind person?

"Here you are, Tim," Teach said, leading Shakespeare into a neat room where a teenager, with a scowl blacker than Tessa's worst, sat hunched and glowering on the edge of a bed.

"Your dog is Shakespeare, a yellow Lab. Hey, that's a good match! Mr. Shakespeare, meet Mr. Browning."

Tim Browning did not smile. Shakespeare had never heard of Robert Browning, the poet, but he knew Teach was making a joke. Not a very good one to judge by Tim's scowl.

"I'm sorry," the guy on the bed growled, not glancing at Shakespeare. "Coming here to get a dog was not my idea. I'm only giving it a shot to satisfy my family...well, my father really. My mother knows it's a mistake too. She takes me places, and we manage just fine. I'm better off as I am. I don't even like dogs much."

Teach was not smiling, but he still sounded friendly.

"Hey, laddie, give us a chance, now you're here," he said quietly. "I think I can promise that this particular dog will grow on you. I've trained a lot of these mutts and cared about every one of them, but Shakespeare is the smartest. He seems to get my meaning almost right away. I think you'll really enjoy him. He is a vanilla dog with caramel ears."

"Who cares what he looks like? I'm not going to be seeing him," Tim muttered.

Teach went on as if he had not caught the interruption. "He weighs sixty-eight pounds. Call him."

The boy's lips clamped together in a thin line.

"Come on, guy. It isn't Shakespeare's fault you hate the world and everyone in it," Teach said.

Shakespeare decided not to wait. He trotted over and leaned against Tim's knees. The boy shrank back.

Teach shrugged his shoulders and leaned down to stroke the dog's head. Then he spoke quietly.

"He'll help you live a full life if you let him. I'll leave you now to get to know each other. See you at Park Time."

What on earth is Park Time? Shakespeare wondered.

"That's when we take them out to pee, right?" the young man muttered.

"You got it," Teach said and left dog and master alone.

When Shakespeare heard the latch click, he wanted to throw back his head and howl the way he had done at the Bensons' when Tessa had shut her bedroom door in his face on that awful first afternoon. But he was not

19

a baby anymore. He stared at the door that Teach had closed and whined softly.

Teach's footsteps grew fainter until the sound of them faded from even Shakespeare's sensitive ears. Whining had not worked. Well, he was not surprised. Teach was no softie.

What's more, Teach expected him to change this grouch's life. How? Well, it was obvious how he must start. Make friends. He sighed. Then he plodded back to stand next to the bed. He sighed again, louder, and licked the hand that lay on Tim's knee. The young man snatched it away as though he had been bitten to the bone.

"Listen, dog, and listen good," he snarled. "I don't need you, and I don't want you. Leave me alone. Go count your toenails or something."

Shakespeare had been through this with Tessa, but she had been just a kid, easy to win over, easy to forgive. This big guy was a jerk. Shakespeare flopped down next to the bed and cleaned his paws. He needed some thinking time.

What had Teach meant about his helping

this Tim have a full life? Why should he? And what was a "full life" exactly?

Tim had flung himself down on the bed, turned his back and buried his face in the pillow. He was making a queer gulping noise. Shakespeare stood up again to take a closer look.

The guy was crying!

Shakespeare stared at his long, gangly body. Wasn't he too big to cry like this? He sounded...scared and lonely...and mad.

Well, it was time to try again. Teach was trusting him to be smart. He put his paws on the bed and nosed the strip of bare back that showed between Tim's jeans and his shirt.

The boy yelped and shot up into a sitting position. It was better than crying.

"Hey, quit that!" Tim shouted.

But something else was wrong. The boy still wasn't looking at Shakespeare. His next words flabbergasted the puzzled dog.

"Where are you?" Tim asked.

Shakespeare backed away and stared. For twenty heartbeats he waited for Tim's eyes to discover him. When they didn't, he charged

back at a gallop and thrust his muzzle right into Tim's lap. Tim tried to fend him off, but he was no longer so angry.

I've seen him cry, Shakespeare thought. He knows I know how he hurts inside.

"It's not your fault," Tim Browning told the dog in a voice just above a whisper. "It's not your fault that I don't want you. I don't want anybody. I'm seventeen, and as far as I'm concerned my life is over. I'd kill myself except I can't do that to my family. It would destroy Betsy. She's only nine."

He hadn't been pretending to cry. Tears were rolling down his cheeks. Shakespeare leaned in and licked them away. All at once, he knew what "blind" meant. Tim's eyes were open, but they were not seeing. He looked as though he was staring straight at the wall, but the dog could tell he wasn't seeing it either. Blind! Like Teach with the blindfold—only for Tim the blindfold could not be whisked away.

And Teach was counting on him, Shakespeare, to help the poor guy pull out of his funk.

Shakespeare couldn't fix the blindness. But he nosed Tim's hand again, just letting him know a dog was there and on his side. Tim was like Larkin, a bit of a wimp, but Shakespeare had pulled Larkin around. This one would be tougher. But Shakespeare had been trained by Teach. And Teach would go on helping him. He wished he knew who Betsy was. She sounded important.

How should he begin? First, keep trying to make friends. That had worked with Tessa. And Teach would help him do the rest. Suddenly all the schooling he had been given made perfect sense. He was to guide this young man, keep him safe, make him laugh and, he told himself, have fun while he was at it.

Tim Browning had an awful lot to learn before he would be ready to leave the Seeing Eye, Shakespeare decided, studying the glum face.

The dog got to work. By the time Teach yelled "Park Time" down the hall, Shakespeare had clowned around so successfully that Tim had had to choke back one feeble laugh. Hearing that laugh was as good as winning a race with Skip. Better even.

And tomorrow, Shakespeare and his "blind person" would be on the street training together. What if a car came too close and scared the young man so badly that he would not go on?

Not on Maple Street, Shakespeare told himself. Not with Teach and me.

# Chapter 4

It wasn't quite as simple as Shakespeare had imagined. That very night, the dog heard his new master crying again in the darkness. Shakespeare knew what was wrong now; he could smell the boy's fear. But it worried the boy far more than the dog. The Lab was certain that once Tim got outside with him and the instructor, he would forget his over-whelming anxiety.

Shakespeare lay and listened to the muffled sobs. Maybe he should jump up on the bed and nuzzle Tim's neck or ear. But Tessa had said that Seeing Eye dogs were not allowed up on beds. He would wait a day and see if things improved.

He wore his harness to breakfast. Tim gripped the handle so tightly that he would be unlikely to feel any message Shakespeare sent him. But it didn't matter. Not yet.

"Loosen up your hand there, Tim," Teach called quietly as they passed. "You two look great together."

Tim jumped as though he had had an electric shock. He stopped in his tracks and half-turned to where the voice had come from.

"Keep going," Teach urged. "You're holding up the parade. Give him the forward command and don't forget to pour on the praise."

Tim stood stock-still until his dog shifted, wagging his tail furiously against the boy's leg. It was as though Shakespeare had pressed an ON switch.

"Forward, Shakespeare," Tim said, his voice unsteady.

Shakespeare obeyed smoothly, his tail still signaling happiness. He was not only sending Tim a message; he was saying "Hi" to Teach. The instructor grinned and waved at him.

All the students undid their dogs' harnesses and coaxed the animals to lie down under the table. Some of the dogs would not settle, but Shakespeare lay still as a statue except for the tip of his tail, which twitched happily. People brought in wonderful food for breakfast. One lady tried to share her toast with her dog and was firmly told to keep human food for humans.

"A letter came for you, Timothy," Teach said. "If you put it in your pocket, I'll read it to you when we've finished breakfast."

Tim snatched the envelope so roughly that it crumpled.

"It's from someone called Betsy," Teach said quietly. "I think she has not written many letters yet. Treat it with respect, Timothy."

The frown cleared from Tim's face. "She's my little sister. She's nine," he said. "I thought it would be from my mother."

He sure likes this Betsy, Shakespeare thought, peering up at his new master.

"You'll be on First Trip, Tim," Teach said as calmly as though he were discussing the weather. "Meet me at the front door in fifteen minutes."

Shakespeare was glad that they would be in the first bunch to go out to train. They wouldn't have to wait long. He knew waiting would be torture for Tim.

"Shall we read your letter first?" Teach asked.

"Sure," Tim said gruffly.

"Dear Tim," Teach read, "I hope your dog is great. I miss you. Mom says don't worry if it is too hard for you. I told her it would not be. Write me the dog's name and every-thing. I can't wait to see the two of you. Love, Betsy."

Teach handed the letter back with a chuckle. "She sounds like a great kid," he said.

"She is," Tim said. He sounded surprised, as though he had not thought about his little sister much before her letter came.

"Okay. Let's go," the instructor said.

As calmly as though he had been a dog guide for years, the Lab led his new master down to the front door. The other guy in the van chattered, but Tim said not a word. His knuckles were white. Shakespeare leaned against him, doing his best to be comforting. He could tell that all the first-timers had jitters, but Tim showed it most. He was the youngest. Maybe that was part of it.

"You're first, Tim. Get out of the van and harness him up."

Tim clambered out awkwardly and, with Teach hovering over him a bit, got Shakespeare into harness.

"Take your time," the instructor said quietly.

Finally dog and man were settled side by side. Tim held the harness handle in his left hand with the leash threaded through his fingers.

"Okay. Give him the command 'Forward.' I'll be right behind you."

Tim sucked in a big breath. Through the harness handle, Shakespeare could feel his hand shaking. Tim cleared his throat. "Shakespeare, forward," he mumbled.

Shakespeare walked forward at a steady pace. Tim faltered but soon kept up well. As the two of them moved, the dog could hear Tim gasp as though he could not believe that he was really traveling along on his own, without holding on to someone's arm.

Then Shakespeare stopped.

Tim let out the breath he had been holding. "What did I do wrong?" he asked in a half-frantic voice.

"Slide your right foot forward, Tim," Teach told him calmly.

Shakespeare could see his smile, and Tim could hear it in his voice. Tim slid his foot out. It hit the curb.

"Oh my!" he whispered.

"Praise him, Tim. Give him a pat too. He's doing a great job and so are you," Teach said.

Joy filled Shakespeare all the way to the tip of his waving tail.

That first walk was so simple any baby could have done it. All the turns were to the right, and they merely went around a long rectangle. For Shakespeare, it was a cinch. For Tim Browning, it was a challenge and a journey into freedom.

Tim was too busy keeping his fingers in the right place, remembering the commands, praising his dog and standing up straight to speak to his dog or his instructor about his astonished delight. But the dog knew. He signaled Tim's joy to his trainer, and when he glanced back for a fleeting second he caught Teach's answering grin.

Once Tim was back in the van, however, the young man could not contain himself.

"I did it," he babbled as Mitch and Larkin climbed out and prepared to go on their first walk together. "Well, Shakespeare and I did it. I couldn't believe it. It was like flying."

"We'll be back soon," Teach said. "Okay, Mitch."

"Maybe...just maybe, it'll work," Tim whispered to his dog as the others departed. "Maybe we can go places and do things, boy." He was still babbling as Teach headed the van back to the Seeing Eye.

"I haven't gone anywhere on my own at that pace since...since my accident," he told the others in the lounge. "I had no idea it would feel like that."

"You all did well," Teach said, pleased with them but not surprised. After all, he had been training their dogs for four months. And lots of others before that.

At lunch Shakespeare found himself under the same table with Skip, Larkin and Regis.

*Hey, we're Seeing Eye dogs,* Skip said. *I like it.*

*Me too,* Shakespeare said.

The next few days were like his first days with Teach except it was Tim who was getting the training. In spite of all the reassuring things Teach said, the dog knew his master was still anxious.

On the third day, Tim misjudged the height of a curb, tripped and came down heavily on one knee, ripping his pants.

"It happens to sighted people too," Teach said calmly, hauling him up again and handing him the leash, which he had dropped. "If it happens again, and it well might, do your level best to hang onto the leash. If your dog gets confused or alarmed and takes off, you could find yourself in trouble. Your dog, as I told you, is special, and I cannot imagine him deserting you, but still...hold on."

Shakespeare, true to his reputation for brilliance, had not strayed from the spot, and Teach leaned down and gave him a private scratch behind his left ear.

Tim was mortified by what had happened and went on and on about how dumb he had been until Teach told him to cut it out.

"Everyone has moments like that," he said. "There's no need to make a big deal out of it."

Tim's cheeks darkened, and he turned his head so Teach would not see his face flush. He did not mention tripping again.

"Teach tells me you two make a great team," Mitch told him when they were in the van, waiting for the instructor to finish a trip with Bernice and Amy.

"He does?" Tim said faintly. If he had been a dog, he would have wagged his tail.

Then, two days later, Tim didn't notice that Shakespeare had stopped for a curb and stepped out without waiting. He was thrown off balance, and although he did not fall, he pulled Shakespeare after him as he staggered forward into the lane of traffic. The oncoming car swerved and missed him, but the driver swore as Shakespeare jerked his master back to safety. Tim was not only deeply embarrassed by this close call; his new confidence was also badly shaken. At first he thought the incident had been Shakespeare's fault, but Teach pointed out that the dog had been standing still on the curb until he was yanked forward by his inattentive master.

"You have to pay attention to him," the man warned. "Most accidents, even those that happen to sighted people, happen as a result of a failure to concentrate."

"I could have been killed," Tim wailed. "My mother said it was expecting too much of a dog...Maybe she was right."

"Hey, laddie, cool your jets," Teach said. "Everyone has these small setbacks. The two of you are doing a magnificent job together."

"Oh, I know it isn't Shakespeare's fault," Tim began.

"Enough. Concentrate," Teach rapped out

as Tim came close to hitting a passing woman with his free arm.

But everything was wonderful when, a week later on the Elm Street route, they faced their trial by fire and became a legend.

As they reached Elm itself, Shakespeare found the corner blocked by two men deep in a conversation. Sam and Skip were to his left and due to turn first. He saw a girl passing who looked something like Tessa and was distracted for a split second.

"Shakespeare, forward," Tim said.

Shakespeare realized afterward that he should have obeyed Tim's hand signal, which told him to turn left. Instead he stepped into the street and began to cross seven lanes of traffic. He was a little surprised but not at all worried. Morristown drivers were used to guide dogs, after all, and he, Shakespeare, knew how to jerk his master to safety if he had to.

The first two lanes were clear so he walked on without any correction from Tim. Then a car came up behind them, and Shakespeare heard his master give a horrified gasp. Well, it was too late to turn back. Young man and dog marched on.

Then Shakespeare spotted a large truck bearing down on them. It was time to jump, fast. If only Tim kept his cool and trusted his dog.

# Chapter 5

As the giant vehicle thundered down on them, Shakespeare and Tim leaped back as one being. The truck passed inches in front of them. The driver yelled, and Shakespeare sneezed as the exhaust filled his nostrils.

But he did not turn back. They were past halfway now, and neither of them had suffered a scratch.

Out of the corner of his eye, the dog saw Teach dodging through the traffic as though he were running a race. What was wrong with him? His face was white.

He should trust me, Shakespeare thought, his tail waving jauntily. Tim and Teach might be anxious, but he was enjoying himself.

He paused while another car screeched to a stop near them. Was it stopping or coming on? Stopping. He moved forward again.

"Good boy, Shakespeare," Tim said. His voice trembled.

Shakespeare pricked up his ears, pleased with the praise. Calmly he crossed the second-last lane. Elm Street was wide, all right, but nothing a trained Seeing Eye dog couldn't take in his stride. To Tim, the journey went on for at least a year. But Tim's dog was delighted with the challenge. When Tessa said he would have adventures, she knew what she was talking about. Then, all at once, they had reached the other side. Shakespeare stepped up onto the curb.

"Well, well," Teach's voice said a moment later. "Did you realize, Timothy, that you just crossed Elm safely? Seven lanes. I would have had a heart attack if it had been any dog but Shakespeare. Now do you trust your dog?"

Tim gave a huge sigh of relief. "I do," he said. "But he needn't have gone to so much trouble to show me how smart he is."

"I agree entirely," Teach said with a laugh. "Watching the two of you was torture! It was also great!"

After that, Tim and Shakespeare rode in elevators, went through revolving doors, rode a train to New York City and took a subway ride followed by a dash up twelve blocks past every distraction ever invented. They made it past scaffolds, a million taxis all honking at each other, fruit stands, a woman pushing twins in an enormous carriage, three Pomeranians being walked by a bored hotel employee, ladders, a man backing up while he studied the sky, a gigantic tomcat who regarded all dogs as sworn enemies, and two boys on skateboards. It was a stressful afternoon, but Shakespeare had the time of his life.

"You are magnificent, dog," Tim told him. "How could I have imagined I did not want you?"

They were about to come close to being parted forever.

# Chapter 6

Only two days were left before the dogs were due to go home with their blind owners when the disaster took place.

Skip's master was an older fellow called Sam. He worked in a bank, and he was out of shape. Tim often had to slow down to let Sam catch up.

Bit by bit, in the weeks they had spent at the Seeing Eye, the young man and the older one had become good friends. Sam had been blind for years, but he had never had a guide dog. He had done fine with his white cane. Then he had caught the toe of his shoe in the open end of an iron pipe someone had left on the sidewalk and had fallen flat on his face. He had landed so hard he had broken his two front teeth. His wife had pointed out that a dog would have prevented the accident.

"Our twins told me to get a dog too," he said with a laugh. "We can't have pets where we live, but I could have a Seeing Eye dog, of course. The boys are pretty sharp even if they're only seven. My wife egged them on."

"You must have still had your sight when you met her," Tim said flatly.

"No," Sam said, surprised. "I was born blind. What made you think I had ever been sighted?"

Tim was silent. Shakespeare, noting his stunned expression, was pleased with the way the conversation was going. Sam did not wait for Tim to answer but went on talking about his family. The younger man listened with growing excitement to Sam's stories about his blind friend who loved to ski, his own enjoyment of bowling, his mastery of the Internet and his tales of travel. He also read bits aloud from the letters his twins wrote to him in Braille.

Tim was beginning to believe that you could be blind and enjoy life. Soon he was discussing possible plans with Teach and some of the other students. Shakespeare had been worried that he and his master would hide away inside a house when they got home, but now he began to look forward to their active life together. Then it happened. The dogs were off leash while the two men played cards and talked in Sam's room. Finally, just before midnight, Tim got up to go.

"I'll put the glasses back in the bathroom," he said.

While he was in there, Skip stood up to stretch. Shakespeare could not believe his eyes when his own master, whom he had grown to love, came out, picked up his harness and slipped it over Skip's head.

The dogs stared at each other. They then did their best to straighten the men out. But Tim and Sam had had a long day.

"Your dog must be jealous of Shakespeare," Tim told Sam, shoving his own dog's head away. "Go on, Skipper. You don't come with me, you idiot."

"Here, boy," Sam said, catching hold of Shakespeare. He snapped the bed chain onto Tim's dog's collar. Shakespeare was attached to his wall.

"Good night, man and dog," Tim said. "Forward, Shakespeare."

Skip did his best not to move. He tried to dig in his claws. But the floor was too smooth.

"Leave it! Come on," Tim said. Shakespeare was shocked to see him giving Skip a clumsy leash correction.

Skip kept his feet braced for one more second.

"I said leave it! What's the matter with you?" Shakespeare heard Tim asking Skip, who gazed back helplessly as he was towed down the hall.

Shakespeare had trouble sleeping that night. Sam snored, but that was not the problem. Skip must be sleepless too, he thought. It would all be set right in the morning. It had to be.

Instead it went from bad to worse.

If only it had been one of the other dogs—but Skip was Shakespeare's littermate.

Even Mama had said they were as alike as two chunks of kibble. No human noticed at Park Time. Nobody caught the mistake at breakfast.

"You're on Second Trip, Tim," Teach said.

Shakespeare had been pinning his hopes on his instructor. But the man barely glanced at the two dogs that gazed imploringly up at him.

"Meet me at the front door," he said. "Ten o'clock."

Would they get it straight before they went home? They all knew that they were leaving on Thursday morning, and today was already Tuesday.

"Forward, Shakespeare," Tim said and walked off down the hall with Skip.

Help! thought the real Shakespeare. Please, somebody, help.

# Chapter 7

All morning Shakespeare struggled to make Teach see the mistake. But they were so near the end of the training that Teach didn't pay the kind of attention he had early on.

"I hope Skip is in a better mood by tomorrow," Sam said, shaking his head. "He doesn't feel like himself."

"Your turn to go," Teach said, only half-listening. "You'll be getting a traffic check and there's a loose dog across the street."

Shakespeare had to give all his attention to his work. Sam and Tim both needed to make it to the opposite curb in safety if he were ever to get to go home with his blind master. The whole long day was the same.

"Something's wrong with Shakespeare," Tim told Teach in a worried voice. "He's sluggish."

"He looks fine," the instructor said, not noticing Skip's un-domed brow. He was watching another dog angle the crossing. Tim did not mention his dog again.

Night came and they were still switched. Shakespeare was desperate. He didn't want to go home with Sam. He liked the man, but he belonged to Tim.

That evening they all met back in Sam's room. The men were complaining about their day. Finally Tim said, "Shakespeare even seems to have forgotten where his toys are. Usually he stands by the dresser and waits for me to get out his ball or his Kong. But not today."

"When did they start acting weird?" Sam began.

Suddenly Tim lunged over to Sam's bed and got hold of Shakespeare's head. His dog licked him madly and wagged his tail like an airplane propeller.

Tim let out a great whoop of joy. He hugged his dog, dragging him right up onto his lap and holding the squirming, sprawling body tight.

"You stole my dog!" he bellowed at his friend. "THIS is Shakespeare, you idiot. Skip is his brother, remember? They must look like twins."

"They sure feel alike," Sam said, chuckling, "although there's something different about the shape of their heads. I felt it, but I thought I was crazy."

The reunion was ecstatic. Shakespeare was so relieved he forgot all the manners he had learned at the Seeing Eye. He leaped on and off the bed. He reversed himself and tried to jump right over it in one go. He landed upside down on the mat where he had slept the night before.

"Let's not tell the others," Tim said. "They'll never let us forget it."

"Too late," Teach's voice said. "I was in my room when it dawned on me what might have happened. Dogs have gotten mixed up before, but never for this long. You are right. The two of them do look like twins, but their natures are quite different. It sometimes seems as if

Shakespeare understands English. He even seems to laugh at my jokes. Believe me, he's laughing now!"

He was absolutely right. Shakespeare could feel himself grinning.

"How come you didn't knock?" Sam demanded huffily.

"No secrets are safe when blind men leave their doors open," Teach said.

In fifteen minutes, even Sam and Tim were laughing sheepishly at their monumental error. Only Shakespeare himself seemed to realize that Skip's and his lives were almost changed forever. That was when he knew that he could not bear to lose his master. They were a team. They belonged together.

On Thursday morning, Shakespeare went out on his last trip with Teach. It was just a walk along Morristown's streets. Shakespeare was guiding perfectly, expecting a final exciting traffic check, when he glanced across the street and saw Tessa. He stopped cold.

"Hup, hup," Tim urged automatically. He did not know that a girl was gazing at them.

He had never met her, although Shakespeare had heard Teach reading him a letter about his year at the Bensons'. He looked again. They were all there, Mr. and Mrs. B. and Kevin, even Martha, who had taken them to the Benson farm when they were pups and brought them back a year later.

Shakespeare held his head up so that Tessa would be proud of him and so they would all know their time spent on him had been worth it. His tail wagged hard and fast. He tried not to, but he kept looking over at his girl.

"Leave it, boy," Tim said sharply.

He couldn't guess that his dog was longing to tear over to his old friends.

Tessa was crying, but she was grinning too.

Then Shakespeare saw Larkin coming toward them. Perfect!

*Did you see them?* Larkin yipped.

He got a leash correction and so did Shakespeare when he answered, but it was worth it. Teach told Tim not to worry. Some people the dogs knew were passing.

"Oh, should we stop?" Tim asked.

"Wave and keep going," Teach said, patting Tim on the back.

They returned to the Seeing Eye and finished packing.

What would life be like with Tim? No Teach. No Sam and Skip. No Larkin. But Shakespeare would be a Seeing Eye dog with an important job to do. He had no way of knowing that their first adventure would happen before the plane got off the ground.

"Good-bye," Tim called out the van window. He and Shakespeare were on an early flight. Leaving wasn't easy, but it was exciting. Shakespeare was not only leaving the Seeing Eye and New Jersey; he was leaving the United States too.

"I hope you like being a Canadian dog," Tim had said.

Shakespeare hoped so too. If all Canadians were like Tim, it would be fine. He followed Teach into the airport. At security a flight attendant was ready to take over.

Teach bent to pat Shakespeare.

"You did understand every word I said to you, didn't you, boy?" he said softly, looking deep into the dog's eyes.

Shakespeare nodded his head up and down in a way dogs don't. Would the man get it?

"I thought so," Teach said with a smile. "Have fun, you two."

He was gone. Shakespeare felt lost for an instant. Then he glanced up at his master's face; his own lost feeling was mirrored there. Tim's lips trembled and he looked pale.

The moment had arrived. It was time for Shakespeare to turn into a mature and brilliant Seeing Eye dog. Teach was no longer standing by to give helpful directions. His master and he were on their own.

"Can you just follow me?" the flight attendant said.

It seemed like no time before they were following another flight attendant down the narrow aisle to their seats.

"Here you go—14D," he said.

A squat lady in pink was already sitting in 14C. She took one look at Tim and

Shakespeare and screeched, "Keep that brute away from me! Dawgs aren't allowed on planes."

Shakespeare stared at her, wide-eyed with astonishment.

"He's very gentle," Tim began, going red to the roots of his hair.

"He's a Seeing Eye dog," the flight attendant put in.

"He looks vicious. I was bitten when I was three by a dawg just like him," she shrilled, her beady eyes glaring. "Besides, I'm allergic. I can't eat bananas either. So there!"

Shakespeare was certain she was no such thing. He longed to mouth her elbow a little, but he checked himself for Tim's sake.

"It is quite all right, madam," the flight attendant said smoothly. "I have room for the gentleman and his beautiful dog in First Class."

"I'll move," the lady began, starting to get up.

"No need," the attendant said, smiling. "There will be more legroom there for Shakespeare. Come on, Timothy."

"Shakespeare," the woman echoed blankly. Nobody explained.

They got seated.

Keeping his rump firmly planted on the floor, Shakespeare shifted until he got a paw onto Tim's knee. He gave the tense fingers a comforting lick.

"Down, Shakespeare," Tim commanded.

Shakespeare jerked his offending paw down instantly and watched a smile tug at the corners of Tim's mouth. Good. He had started on his life's work.

# Chapter 8

When the plane was airborne, Shakespeare decided to sleep.

"Would he like a drink of water?" the attendant asked, smiling down at him.

"No, thanks. He's fine," Tim said firmly.

"It's no trouble," she pressed on. "The air gets dry during flight, you know."

"Maybe," Tim replied, his tone pleasant but still firm. "But I can't take him out for a walk up here. So he'll wait. He's a good waiter, aren't you, Shakespeare?"

Shakespeare fluttered his eyelashes to show he heard, but kept his eyes closed to show he was not in the mood to converse. The grand name worked its magic and distracted her. Two other people offered him a pretzel, but Tim stuck to his guns. Shakespeare tried not to let him down by drooling.

Then they were circling above Toronto.

It wasn't long before they were on the ground and the passengers began to file off. Many, spotting the dog for the first time, marveled that they had never once been aware he was on the flight.

"What a beauty she is!" one lady cooed.

"He's a male," Tim corrected her, resting his hand on Shakespeare's head so nobody could pet him without his master knowing.

Man and dog waited for the other people to get off first, as they had been instructed. Staying still was hard for them both, but they pretended to be calm.

The flight attendant then led them to the door and handed them over to a far-from-calm young passenger agent.

"I've never done this before," he said, not looking at Tim. "I'm not sure..."

Tim had been told to go "sighted guide" so his brand-new dog would not be too stressed. But the agent seemed in far worse shape than Shakespeare, and Tim was dying to try walking with his dog guide unsupervised. This must be how a mother feels when she brings her newborn baby home from the hospital, he thought.

"You go ahead," he instructed the jittery young man as though he had been doing it for years. "He'll follow. His name is Shakespeare."

"Does he have to know my name first?" the young man asked.

Tim could not keep from laughing.

"I don't think so," he said. "What is your name?"

"Brandon."

"Shakespeare, this is Brandon. Follow Brandon," Tim Browning said solemnly.

The dog guided flawlessly. It was a heady moment. They were on their own, and they knew exactly what to do.

But Brandon kept dropping back.

Shakespeare slowed down each time and waited for him to move forward. What was wrong with him? They needed him to lead, not to follow.

"We're coming to steps," the agent gasped. "You'd better take my arm now."

"You just keep going," Tim said. "Shakespeare will show me the steps when we get there."

Brandon went right on peering back at them all the way, watching the dog as though he was some sort of explosive device. Suddenly it was too much for him. As they neared the steps, he leaped back, banged into Tim and grabbed hold of the harness handle, jerking Shakespeare sideways.

Tim grunted, lost his balance and almost plunged down the entire flight.

"You see! He wasn't going to stop," Brandon bleated. "I know what you said, but he was not even slowing down."

That was when Shakespeare learned that blind people can glare just as hotly as sighted ones. Tim turned on the man a look that made him back up hastily.

"Get your hands off my dog and watch," he snarled.

He took two steps back and said, "Shakespeare, forward."

Brandon was shaking like jelly but frozen in place. Shakespeare walked straight to the edge of the top step and halted. His master slid his right foot forward, checked the spot and said, "Good boy, Shakespeare. Forward."

Without hesitating, he and his dog began to descend.

Brandon was subdued as he took the young man and his new dog guide through immigration and customs.

"Good luck with him," the customs man said. "He's a handsome fellow."

"Thanks," Tim said in a distracted voice. Now they had his luggage, it was time to meet up with his family.

"I wish I could see their faces," he muttered half under his breath.

Brandon escorted them toward the barrier behind which people were lined up, waiting. But Tim was not paying attention to the agent any longer; he was listening for familiar voices.

As if he had spoken his wish aloud, a shrill voice cried out, "Oh, Timmy, he is absolutely GORGEOUS!"

Tim gave a rueful grin.

"Brace yourself, dog," he muttered. "That's my mother, and I have a feeling she's going to make life difficult for us. You can lead us out to them, Brandon."

But Mrs. Browning had ducked under the barrier and rushed forward to clasp Tim in her arms.

# Chapter 9

"Don't touch him, Mom," Tim said as she stooped to include Shakespeare in her greeting. "He's working right now. Wait until we get home and he's out of harness."

Tim's father, a tall, skinny man who looked like Tim only older, watched the reunion, but he and the child with him stayed behind the barrier until the others came out to them. He grinned down at the yellow Lab standing by his son. He was smiling at his wife.

"Do what he tells you, Eve. He's grown up now," he said quietly.

A girl of about nine was with them. Shakespeare did not need to be told that this was Tim's little sister. Tim had had her picture standing on his dresser at the Seeing Eye.

She did not try to pet her brother's dog, but she did jump up and down with excitement. Her long, dark braids tied with perky bows flew up and down with every jump, and her face wore a beaming smile.

"Hi, hi, hi," she sang out.

"Hi, Betsy," Tim answered, reaching his free arm to hug her.

"Don't call her Betsy," Tim's mother snapped. "Her name is Bethany."

"I like it," Betsy protested.

Her mother ignored this. "Bethany, you heard your brother. Do not touch his precious dog."

Bethany put her hands behind her back and went down on her knees.

"Hi, Shakespeare," she said softly. "I'm Bethany. You can call me Betsy. Tim does."

"Do get up, Bethany. You're in everybody's way," her mother said. She still sounded annoyed, but Shakespeare saw that she was blinking back tears. He himself never shed tears, but his months with Tessa had taught

him to understand them, and his heart soft-
ened a bit toward Mrs. Browning. He sensed
that she did not want to let Tim grow up. He
was her first puppy after all. Even though
Shakespeare knew that her kind of mother-
ing was bad for Tim, she clearly loved him.

Mrs. Browning's attitude was hard for a
dog to understand. His mama had been
proud when they grew strong and stood on
their own paws and ate out of a dish. Once
when Stormy had tried to nurse after she
was able to lap water just fine, Mama had
pushed her away. Humans were sometimes
very strange.

"I'm just introducing myself," Betsy told
her mother in a dignified voice.

Shakespeare loved the little girl from the
first moment of their meeting. What a great
kid!

But the brand-new dog guide did not forget
who his person was. He led Tim Browning
out of the airport without a hitch.

As they drove along, Tim's mother sneaked
her hand back between the bucket seats to
stroke Shakespeare's head. She had a smirk

on her face like a naughty child getting away with something forbidden. After all, Tim couldn't see, and she wasn't hurting this lovely creature. She had forgotten Bethany.

"Mom, don't," the little girl said, shocked.

"Well, you've picked a lovely day to come home on," Mrs. Browning said loudly, making a face at her daughter. "What do you plan to do next? Have a long rest, I hope. It's what you badly need, darling, after all you have been through. Bethany can walk the dog for you."

"No," Tim said quietly. "I walk my own dog. We are a team. Also, I'm in great shape. I've walked miles every day for a month."

"Wow!" Betsy said.

"I have made plans, though," Tim said. "I'm going to finish high school first and then go on to college."

"Sounds good, " said his father.

"College! How can you?" shrieked his mother. "That's out of the question. You can't read or..."

She broke off abruptly and reached in her bag for a Kleenex.

"What college will you go to?" asked Betsy, as though she had not heard her mother's objection. Tim also chose to ignore his mother and respond to his little sister.

"I can live at home and go to the U. of G.," he said. "I know my way around there more or less. And I think they'll have the courses I'm interested in."

He paused to take a deep breath and then spoke to his mother.

"I've thought it all out, Ma. Lots of blind people go to college. Helen Keller did—and she was deaf *and* blind. I just have to pick up some new skills. You should have met some of the people at the Seeing Eye. Plenty of them had college degrees."

"Goody," Betsy said. "I like you being home."

Shakespeare grew thoughtful. He would go to college too, of course. But what was "college" exactly? And what were Tim's "interests"?

Also, he thought he had better get busy looking out for a mate for his master or that mother of his might ruin everything that Teach had tried to encourage in Tim.

The Seeing Eye had told the new dog owners to keep their dogs on leash for the first two weeks to help them to bond and to understand their new environment Everyone, Shakespeare included, had trouble with this. Tim was a tall young man, and his dog was also large. They kept getting hung up on the furniture and tangled with the people. But Tim was determined to make it work.

As soon as they got home, he fed Shakespeare since the dog had gone without a meal before the flight. Then he announced in a voice that he tried to keep light, "Okay. I'm taking him out to relieve himself, and then we'll go for a walk."

"I can't come with you right now," his mother said, flustered and tense. "I have to get supper started. Bethany…"

"No. I want to go by myself," Tim said. "I won't go far, and I promise I won't get lost. I'm sorry, but Betsy would be a distraction right now. We won't be gone long."

He put Shakespeare's harness back on and followed him out the door. They walked around in circles in the yard while Tim chanted, "Park time, boy. Hurry up."

Shakespeare felt embarrassed and slightly confused at first, but he did need to pee so he got on with it.

As they went out the gate and headed down the sidewalk, Shakespeare heard the gate opening and closing again. He glanced back. Tim's mother was creeping after them. The dog stopped in his tracks and looked back.

"I heard her," Tim muttered. He turned and called over his shoulder. "Go home, Mother, or we won't move from this spot. Can't you see that you're breaking Shakespeare's concentration by shadowing us?"

"But what if..." Mrs. Browning began.

"LEAVE US ALONE!" Tim shouted at her, his patience snapping. "I am an adult man, and I don't want my mother checking up on my every move. You might as well hire a nanny."

Mrs. Browning turned and scuttled back through the gate.

"Forward, Shakespeare," Tim said. His voice and his hands were unsteady.

Shakespeare set out, calmly, steadily guiding. It was a lovely afternoon, and he was having fun. He tried to make Tim notice the sunlight and feel the soft wind blowing in their faces. They were together, and they were a team, just the way Teach had promised.

In five minutes, they had gone around the block.

"Let's cross the street just to prove we can," Tim said. "Then we can go home again. I know it's crazy, but I'm bushed. We can sit on the porch for a while and then try a walk in the other direction."

Shakespeare stopped neatly at the curb. Tim was so rattled that he did not give the command "Forward" for a full fifteen seconds.

"Well, go," he said finally. "Oh, heavens. I mean Forward, Shakespeare."

The dog stepped down off the curb. They crossed without incident. It was a quiet street. Not a single car was in sight. As they came back to the Brownings' house, Shakespeare caught a quick glimpse of Betsy peering out the window. The minute she knew she had been spotted, she ducked out of sight.

Shakespeare wagged his tail extra hard and headed up the front walk. Tim felt around for one of the hammock chairs and plunked himself into it. Two seconds later, Betsy came strolling out.

"Oh, Tim," she said brightly. "I didn't know you were out here."

Then she gave herself away by giggling.

"I didn't follow you," she said hastily. "But I was watching out the window. Shakespeare saw me, didn't you, boy?"

Shakespeare thumped his tail.

"Brad phoned," she went on. "He wanted to know if you were okay."

"What did you tell him, sister dear?" Tim asked.

Shakespeare heard bitterness under the casual question. Betsy must have noticed it too because she sounded nervous when she answered.

"I said you were great, and Shakespeare was gorgeous, and you'd probably give him a call."

Tim did not respond. Shakespeare stood up and went to him. He nosed his master's hand, but Tim did not lift it to scratch behind his ear or stroke him. Who was this Brad anyway?

"I don't think so," Tim said at last in a flat hard voice. "He knows where I am. I doubt we'll have much to say to each other after we've talked about my gorgeous dog. You know and I know that all Brad cares about is football."

"Well, I had to tell him you were home," Betsy said. "Mom talked to him too. She... she might have asked him over."

Tim swore and hoisted himself out of the chair.

"Come on, dog," he growled. "We have more walking to do."

They went faster this time, and Tim almost turned in to someone's front walk, imagining they were at the corner. He figured it out when Shakespeare stopped at the front steps of the house.

"You are a good boy," he said when they were back on track. "But guess what? Being blind is a drag. And even you can't make it good."

Shakespeare knew this was true.

When Tim's old friend Brad did come over with another boy called Tony, they did not know what to say. Mrs. Browning tried to fill up the silence with talk about the weather. Shakespeare longed for Sam from the Seeing Eye to drop by.

Then Tim's first Talking Books came in the mail, and his life was suddenly better. Walking his guide dog around town and losing himself in a good mystery helped fill the empty days. Brad and Tony did not come again.

Two weeks later, Tim started back to school. He had been in the middle of his final year when he had been blinded in a traffic accident. He had had good marks, so the school allowed him to skip repeating all the courses he was halfway through while he worked to become adept on a talking computer and learned to read and write Braille.

"I can go on with my regular classes after

Christmas," Tim told his parents after he spent the morning with someone from the Canadian National Institute for the Blind. "They say there's another blind student who will learn the computer stuff and Braille with me."

"What's his name, and where does he come from?" Mrs. Browning asked at once.

Tim laughed.

"I have no idea," he admitted. "We'll be meeting on Tuesday at the high school, and we'll start on the rest in about ten days when the equipment is delivered and installed. They have a Center for Disabled Students at the university, you know, and they filled in the forms to get me my own computer and speech program. I guess I was so over-whelmed by everything that the guy's name didn't seem important."

Mrs. Browning snorted at this, but Tim's dad laughed. Betsy looked solemn.

"It'll be nice for you to have a friend," she said softly.

"Yeah," Tim agreed, "but we may not get along, Betsy. I met people at the Seeing Eye who were far from kindred spirits. Being blind isn't enough to build a friendship on."

"But he might be great," his little sister insisted. "Does he have a dog?"

"I didn't even ask," Tim said sheepishly. "But I did find out I can take an English course in the afternoons, a course in Shakespeare! How about that, boy?"

The following Wednesday afternoon, Shakespeare found himself lying under Tim's desk and hearing the English teacher saying, "Shakespeare's clowns are among his most interesting characters."

Tessa had told him that the first Shakespeare had been a famous writer long ago. He had written stuff: "To pee or not to pee...that is the question." She had called him Will sometimes. And now Tim did too.

None of this worried Shakespeare, but something else did. It even kept him awake at night. He was worried about Tim's plan to walk up the hill to the university.

Mr. Browning had driven them up at first because there was a lot to arrange and

Tim had to memorize the route. His father had stuck around and driven them home too. But from the car window Shakespeare had glimpsed a river. The very sight of the water as they drove across the bridge made the dog shiver as he remembered his near drowning when he was a pup.

"Tomorrow we're walking," Tim said on Sunday afternoon. "I know the way, after all. Don't fuss, Mom. I'm a big boy."

"But you'll have to cross Wellington," his mother said. "Shakespeare's smart, but face it, darling, he's a dog. That street is dangerous."

She went on and on until Tim got up and stalked out of the room. Shakespeare wished he had been in harness. He could have kept him from tripping over her footstool, which she was forever shifting from place to place.

Tim caught at the doorjamb for balance, slammed the door behind him and banged up the stairs.

Betsy got up and opened the door again quietly so Shakespeare could follow.

"There you go, boy," she said softly.

Giving her a grateful wag, the dog padded after his master. He knew Tim would be sprawled on his bed. Things had not changed that much in six weeks.

# Chapter 10

Tim's gorgeous guide dog lay awake that night, thinking about the journey ahead.

He was not worried about the route. He was worried about the river. The bridge was wide, but would Tim keep away from the edge? Cars drove up and down in the middle.

The next afternoon, he had trouble concentrating as they neared the park where the river ran. But the bridge *was* wide. Even though he had to keep over to the edge, the railing made him feel safe. Still, he fixed his eyes on the sidewalk and went as fast as Tim would let him.

"We should try the footbridge sometime, boy," Tim remarked as he strode along, free from his bevy of hovering human helpers. "The only trouble is that you're a Lab. You'd probably decide to take a swim one day."

Shakespeare knew he would do no such thing. Never, ever! He remembered his tumble into the rushing creek all too clearly, even though it had happened months before. He felt again the choking, the bruises, the terror, the darkness shutting down inside his bursting head. He would never swim again.

Then he saw someone who made him forget his dread of water. A girl and her dog were walking up the street ahead of them. She was beautiful. Maybe the girl was too, but Shakespeare was entranced by the dog. She was small and golden and she wore a harness just like his own.

Shakespeare speeded up, dragging his master behind him.

"Hey, Shakespeare, leave it!" Tim yelled, jerking the leash.

Teach's voice, deep inside the dog's mind, said, "Intelligent disobedience. That's what we teach them. Trust your dog. He'll look after you."

Tim's trustworthy dog ignored the correction. He tore on as fast as he could.

"Phooey!" Tim roared. "Phooey!"

The girl stopped as they came up behind her. Her dog was craning her neck around so she could get a good look at the other dog guides in harness.

"Pippa, quit it," her mistress said. "Or am I right in thinking that we have met the other blind student who's going to be learning Braille along with me?"

"Oh, he's chasing another dog!" Tim said, gasping for breath. "My name's Tim Browning, and he's Shakespeare. I thought the other student was a boy."

Shakespeare edged closer to Pippa. Their people were not noticing. They could get acquainted.

*Has she got a mate already?* Tim's dog asked. It was nice to talk Dog for a change. He'd been with humans night and day for weeks.

*Not yet,* Pippa said softly. *She's shy. Maybe we should move along before they start in with the leash corrections.*

*Right you are,* Shakespeare said.

He switched his ears over to Human to see if Tim needed help.

"I'm Leslie Barrett," the girl was saying. "I need to strengthen my Braille skills before I start working toward my BA. I know Leslie can be taken for a boy's name. I was named after my dad, after all. I've been blind since I was small, but I've attended regular school and done my work with Talking Books and kids who read to me. I decided I want to be independent now I've finished high school. If you can't read and write Braille, you are illiterate."

"Not really," Tim said, starting to walk beside her. "But I know what you mean. You can't leave yourself a message."

When the two of them arrived at the Center for Disabled Students, the young people and their dog guides felt they had known each other for years.

A week later, Tim discovered that the play he was going to be studying was on at the Stratford Festival. At the same time, his mother, who had bought tickets so she could take him and his sister as a surprise, found out that her cousin was flying in from England that evening.

"When is your last class over?" Tim asked Leslie.

"Two o'clock," Leslie said.

Tim's face lit up. "Good," he said.

"Why?" Leslie asked him.

"I have a good idea, but I have to check first," he told her. That night, when the subject of the Stratford Festival came up again, he made a suggestion.

"How about I invite Leslie?" he said.

"I could drive you," his father offered. He was not keen on his wife's relatives.

Betsy cheered and turned a cartwheel.

Shakespeare felt his master's tension through the harness handle as Tim waited to hear whether Leslie would join the party.

"Sure," Leslie said, without an instant's hesitation.

"How about coming over tonight and having supper with us?" Tim suggested, his voice unsteady with eagerness.

"Wonderful!" Leslie said. "One does get tired of eating in residence."

They had a grand time. Not only the humans, but Pippa and Shakespeare also enjoyed themselves. After supper they made detailed plans for their trip to the theater.

"Are you sure you don't want to see the play?" Leslie asked Tim's father.

"I had enough of Shakespeare at school," Mr. Browning said. "He puts me to sleep, and I'm in danger of snoring."

Shakespeare did not take this personally. He looked forward to the expedition, never guessing that Stratford was located on a river where ducks and swans sailed by.

"This is going to be fantastic," Betsy said. "It will be so neat to go with two dogs!"

"It'll be Betsy's tenth birthday that day. And it'll be her first trip to a Shakespearean play," Tim told Leslie.

Mrs. Browning looked concerned, but nobody paid any attention to her.

"It does sound fantastic," Leslie said. She was so at home with her blindness that she astonished Tim's anxious mother. Pippa was clearly happy. Her joyous tail said so. Shakespeare was pleased as punch. Still, nobody had spoken of the Avon River.

# Chapter 11

On Betsy's birthday, Leslie met Tim and his dad outside the Johnson Building after her last class. She was taking a Shakespeare course too. Mr. Browning grinned at Shakespeare as the two students talked.

Betsy loved Leslie and Pippa. She could not decide which one was her favorite. Shakespeare liked Leslie well enough, but he preferred Pippa. It was so relaxing talking Dog. It gave him a chance to complain about Tim's fussbudget mother.

*Leslie's grandma is like that,* Pippa said. *She was sure we couldn't manage living in residence. But Leslie dug her heels in and here we are.*

In Stratford, Betsy and Tim and Leslie said good-bye to Mr. Browning and started down the hill with their picnic supper. Shakespeare was having a lovely time.

Then Betsy said, "I brought dried corn to feed the swans. Bread is bad for them, you know. Mom got it from Wild Birds Unlimited. It's the right food for wild water birds."

Shakespeare stopped in his tracks.

Swans! Water birds! What was Betsy talking about? A cold finger of fear poked deep into him.

Pippa paused to look back at him.

*What's wrong?* she asked softly.

He couldn't tell her.

*Nothing. Nothing at all,* he gulped and started walking again.

"What made him stop?" Betsy asked. "I don't see any danger."

"Teach said, 'Trust your dog!' so I trust him," Tim said, laughing.

Shakespeare trembled. There it was: a river with birds swimming on it. It was much bigger than the creek that had tried to kill him. He braced his paws, refusing to go closer.

"Here's a picnic table," Betsy called, slapping it so the others could find it.

It wasn't right on the riverbank. Shakespeare sighed with relief. Pippa pulled to get nearer the water.

"She swims at our cottage," Leslie said. "I'll keep her harnessed so she won't jump in. I've heard swans can be dangerous if they get roused. Are there really swans, Betsy?"

Tim took off Shakespeare's harness. "He's never been swimming," he said. "And he was in harness all day."

"Oh, yes, there are lots, but they aren't close to us yet," Betsy answered Leslie's question. "There are ducklings, but they are half-grown."

"Let's feed ourselves first," Tim said, opening the picnic supplies.

They ate. Pippa gazed at the river with longing. Shakespeare gazed at the food. Then Betsy took her bag of corn to the water's edge.

Shakespeare sat bolt upright. Tim and Leslie were so busy talking they didn't notice her leaving. He watched her toss the first handful. Two stately swans floated toward her. A lineup of half-grown cygnets paddled after them.

Betsy was thrilled. She tried to throw the grain right to the babies. Her aim went wild, and a handful landed at the river's edge. She leaned forward to scoop up what she could.

*No!* Shakespeare called out in Dog. *Don't, Betsy! Leave it!*

She did not heed him. She bent further forward and lost her balance. With a cry of surprise and fright, she tumbled into the Avon River. If it had not been for the cob swan, she would not have been in danger. The water was shallow, and Betsy was a good swimmer. But the male swan, already nervous about his family, raised his great wings and lowered his head. He hissed horribly and sped straight for Betsy Browning.

Pippa loved water. But she was in harness. Hearing Betsy's cry, Tim and Leslie jumped to their feet. But they were blind. They could never get to Betsy in time. The enraged swan would reach her first.

Shakespeare, certain he would die in the

next few moments, raced to the riverbank and leaped spread-eagled into the water. Betsy, soaked to the skin, was almost back to the edge. Water streamed down her face, but she swiped it out of her eyes with the back of her hand. She stared up at the dog flying through the air above her.

"Shakespeare did a perfect stride-jump," she would tell her brother later. "And it worked. He kept his head above water."

Shakespeare had never heard of a stride-jump. He didn't stop to pull Betsy to safety. He went straight for the charging swan.

A reporter who happened on the scene and wrote it up for the newspaper said that Shakespeare fought the swan off in single combat. Really, in the nick of time, a powerful old lady out for her evening stroll by the Avon thundered to the aid of the gallant dog. She swung her enormous black umbrella at the onrushing bird. The umbrella came unfastened in midair and flapped open and shut in a truly alarming manner. The embattled swan turned on the uncanny, black, bird-like object in her hand. He soon discovered that it was not alive. Seeing his family swimming rapidly away, he smoothed down his ruffled feathers and took off after them, shaken but triumphant.

He was not sure what had happened exactly, but clearly he had won. His mate turned her head and looked back at him admiringly. She appreciated his great bravery. He sailed after her as proudly as a clipper ship with all sails set.

In the meantime, Shakespeare had turned and struck out for shore. Then it dawned on him. He was swimming. He, Shakespeare, the dog who was terrified of even small streams of water, could not only swim, but he swam very well indeed. And, incredibly, he loved the water. He felt as though he had been doing this astonishing thing for years and years. Tim was right all along. He was a water dog. He need never fear water again.

Proud but sopping, he bounced out and shook himself hard. Despite showering everyone near him, he was still wet.

"Eeeek!" Betsy Browning yelped as she was drenched for the second time. Any part of her that had stayed dry after being dunked in the Avon was now soaked along with the rest of her.

Betsy had been doing her best to make a joke out of the disaster, but as Shakespeare doused her she burst into tears. It was too much. She and Tim's dog had ruined everything.

"I'm sorry. I'm sorry," she blubbered. "I didn't mean to. I'm half-drowned, Tim, and I've spoiled everything."

She began to fling herself at him, but he felt her rush and caught her by the arms and held her off.

"Betsy Browning, stop bawling and tell me exactly what has happened," her big brother ordered. "Are you hurt? Is Shakespeare all right?"

"The child was nearly attacked by a cob swan," said the woman with the umbrella. "But that fool bird has taken himself off and your brave dog is fine. The little girl is wet and in shock but not injured. I'm Mrs. Wetherby, by the way."

"She helped scare the swan away," Betsy

burst in. "She whacked at it with her monster umbrella."

"The things we miss!" Tim said to Leslie.

"Shakespeare didn't get hurt," Betsy added. "Just wet. Like me. Thank you for saving us," she added shyly.

"I didn't do much. The dog had already scared off the swan. You'll both dry in no time. I think you still have time before the performance," the old lady said, chuckling.

"I have the towel I take swimming in my backpack," Betsy said, cheering up.


By curtain time, both girl and dog were damp but no longer dripping. Leslie, Tim and Betsy marched into the theater giggling, eyes front, heads high. Betsy did look rumpled and a bit damp around the edges, but if anyone noticed, they were polite enough to say nothing. People did stare, but they always gazed at beautiful dog guides when they were working. On this night, the dogs caught every eye as they led their blind people down the long flight of steps to the orchestra seats.

Throughout the entire play, Shakespeare and Pippa behaved perfectly. Shakespeare enjoyed the whole performance, although he did find some of the words hard to catch. William Shakespeare's Human was more complicated than most, and Shakespeare missed a lot. The story seemed a bit silly. Shakespeare fell asleep during the last act.

"Stick with us, Betsy," Tim said as they came out. "We don't want to lose you in the crowd. Dad's meeting us back at the parking lot."

"I just wish Mom didn't have to know I fell in," Betsy sighed. "She said it might be dangerous to feed the swans."

"We won't tell," Leslie promised, smiling.

"She'll know," Betsy said in a doomed voice. "Or she'll find out. She always does."

Just like Mrs. Benson knew when I fell in the creek, Shakespeare thought, remembering.

At that exact moment, the heavens opened and rain poured down, drenching all the theatergoers, dogs and children included.

"Wonderful!" cried Tim. "Listen, guys. No need to mention Betsy's swim. Mother and Dad will think we're damp because we got caught in the rain."

"And they'll be quite right," Leslie laughed.

They stood in a row, their faces turned up, letting themselves be soaked to the skin and laughing. Older people, raising umbrellas, shook their heads at the foolishness of the young. The dogs shook too, spraying everyone within reach.

"This way, Tim," Mr. Browning called. "Sorry I didn't beat the downpour."

They clambered into the van. "Really, your timing was perfect," Tim said. "We needed a wash."

The next afternoon, Mrs. Browning hunted high and low for the *Guelph Mercury*.

"Has anyone seen the paper?" she asked. "I brought it in from the front porch, but it has vanished."

"Shall I help you look?" Tim asked, teasing.

"Oh, Tim, don't joke about your loss," she said. "I didn't mean…"

"Of course you didn't," he told her. "But it helps me to make light of it."

"You do very well making light of darkness," his father said quietly.

The doorbell rang. Betsy ran to see who it was and came back looking puzzled.

"It's a telegram for Shakespeare," she said, staring at it.

"What next!" her mother snapped. "Well, read it to him."

Betsy bent down close to the Lab and read out the following message:

RESCUE DOG MADE THE MORRIS-TOWN PAPER STOP WELL DONE SHAKESPEARE STOP YOUR FRIENDS AT THE SEEING EYE

"What on earth does it mean?" Mrs. Browning said with a frown. "I don't understand a word of it."

"Perhaps I should read you this after all," her husband said, producing the lost newspaper from behind his back. "Excellent picture. Now listen, everyone."

97

## SHAKESPEARE, A SEEING EYE DOG, SAVES CHILD FROM SWAN ATTACK

*Betsy Browning attended the Stratford Festival yesterday with her brother, Tim, and his guide dog, Shakespeare. When a swan attacked the little girl, the brave dog plunged into the Avon and rescued Betsy from the cob swan in single combat.*

"Betsy, that's you!" her mother cried.

Tim had to tell the whole story then. They tried to play it down, but the picture was a dilly. It showed Betsy in the water and Shakespeare in midair, springing off the bank. It also caught the swan's head. He looked extraordinarily vicious.

"Tim, why weren't you watching her?" their mother cried. "Poor Bethany! Why didn't you phone Dad?"

"Betsy wanted to see the play," Tim said. "You did, didn't you, Bets?"

"I sure did. And it was great. I was perfectly dry by then," Betsy said. "And Shakespeare loved it too, didn't you, boy?"

Shakespeare wagged his tail and smiled at her.

"I thought that dog was supposed to look after *you*, Timothy, not rescue your sister!" Tim's mother said crossly, trying to hide how shaken she was.

"Shakespeare *has* rescued me," Tim said softly. "Over and over. From loneliness, from fear, from dependence."

"Oh, Tim..." his mother broke in, her eyes shining with tears.

"Listen, Mom. You should know what a splendid dog Shakespeare is. My old friends have moved on, but my Seeing Eye dog found Leslie and Pippa for me. He even got a leash correction doing it. And what's more, he not only saved Betsy the other night, but before we met he also helped a guy who was knocked out by a tree limb. He tore away and got the man's wife with her first-aid kit. I heard all about it. He's known far and wide as Shakespeare, Rescue Dog."

Mrs. Browning turned away and blew her nose. Betsy grinned like a jack-o'-lantern and reached to stroke one of the dog's velvet ears. Mr. Browning took the paper back and sat down to read it over again.

Rescue Dog, stretched out at his master's feet, thumped his tail on the carpet again, even harder. He *had* been braver than any of them knew. Little did they know how much he had feared birds and water until he found himself in the river. But it had been fun! Now he had to get to work on them. He was determined to go swimming again. He supposed he would have to teach Tim to understand Dog. It shouldn't be that hard. He was halfway there already.

*Tim,* Shakespeare said in his loudest Dog, *how about taking Pippa and me for a dip?*

Tim stared down at him.

"You know, I could swear Shakespeare is trying to ask me something. What is it, boy?"

"Oh, I can tell you that," Betsy said. "He wants to go swimming."

# Author's Note

I have had three exceptional dogs. The first was called Zephyr. He was in many ways the inspiration for Shakespeare. When we met in Morristown at the Seeing Eye, Zephyr knew fourteen commands. Like Shakespeare he was not at all sure he wanted to belong to me. He had been raised by a family he loved, and then he had been taught his guiding skills by a woman he adored. When he was brought to my room, he went to the door and whined to be let out so that he could go and find her.

But I loved him so much that he finally gave in and came back to Canada with me.

Before he retired when he was ten, he knew thirty-two commands, including such things as "Fetch my shoes." He would bring me one and wait until I said, "And the other one." He was a dog with a great sense of humor. I wrote about him in my book *Stars Come Out Within*, and his picture is on the cover.

When I returned to the Seeing Eye for my second dog guide, I was given a big black Lab who was named Ritz. He was anxious at first and always took his work seriously. I had two tiny Papillons by then, and my sister and her Scottie dog, her granddaughter and later her grandson moved with me into an old farmhouse where Ritz had to use his country training because there were no sidewalks. He managed to get along in that busy house filled with dogs, cats and two young children.

Ritz retired when he was ten and became a family pet, and I returned to the Seeing Eye and came home with my third dog guide, a small yellow Lab named Pippa.

I still have Pippa, although she is now nine and nearly ready to retire. She was named Hula when I got her, and she was raised by a girl named Autumn to whom *Rescue Pup* is dedicated. Pippa is not as serious as Ritz and not as funny as Zephyr, but she is a darling and I will miss having her as my guide.

All of these dogs played a part in *Rescue Pup*, my first book about Shakespeare, and in this one, which tells about what happened when Shakespeare went to school and became a proper Seeing Eye dog. These dogs are wonderful. Each one is different, but all are loving and so proud to be dog guides. I truly believe that my three Seeing Eye dogs have all understood both Dog and Human, the way Shakespeare does.

**Jean Little** is one of Canada's most beloved writers for children. She is also blind and currently living with her third Seeing Eye dog. Three times she has traveled to the Seeing Eye headquarters in New Jersey to train with a dog, first Zephyr, then Ritz and now Pippa. For years she has thought about writing a book about the training of a Seeing Eye dog. Now she has done it, but Shakespeare is not just any dog.

Jean is also the author of *Birdie for Now*, *I Gave My Mom a Castle*, *The Birthday Girl* and *Rescue Pup*. She lives in Guelph, Ontario.

# Orca Young Readers

# Orca Young Readers Series

**Max and Ellie series by Becky Citra**
*Ellie's New Home, The Freezing Moon,*
*Danger at The Landings, Runaway,*
*Strawberry Moon*

**TJ series by Hazel Hutchins**
*TJ and the Cats, TJ and the Haunted House,*
*TJ and the Rockets*

**Basketball series by Eric Walters**
*Three on Three, Full Court Press, Hoop Crazy!*
*Long Shot, Road Trip, Off Season, Underdog,*
*Triple Threat*

**Kaylee and Sausage series by Anita Daher**
*Flight from Big Tangle,*
*Flight from Bear Canyon*